There are lots of days I like throughout the year. But Valentine's Day isn't one of them. Every year my mom goes out and buys valentine cards. Every year we make a valentine box in school. Every year we have a party. And every year, I worry:

WHAT IF I'M THE ONLY KID IN CLASS WHO DOESN'T GET EVEN ONE DUMB VALENTINE CARD?!

Don't you ever worry about that? Even though it has never happened to me, I'm still afraid that it will. This year I decided to do something about it. But I really, really messed things up. If you get bored and want to mess up your Valentine's Day, here's how to do it, step by step.

Happy Valentine's Day (HA! HA!),

WILLIMENA RULES!

RULE BOOK #5
23 Ways to Mess Up Valentine's Day

By Valerie Wilson Wesley
Illustrated by Maryn Roos

JUMP AT THE SUN
HYPERION BOOKS FOR CHILDREN • NEW YORK

For Cheo and Tumani

Text copyright © 2005 by Valerie Wilson Wesley
Illustrations copyright © 2005 by Maryn Roos

For information address Hyperion Books for Children,
114 Fifth Avenue, New York, New York 10011-5690.

Printed in the United States of America

First Edition

1 3 5 7 9 10 8 6 4 2

Library of Congress Cataloging-in-Publication Data on file.

ISBN 0-7868-5524-X

Visit www.jumpatthesun.com

My Rules Step by Step

Willimena's Rules

STEP #1:
Get a Bad Case of the "Blahs"

It was a boring time of year. Everything fun had already happened. Thanksgiving and Christmas were over. We'd celebrated Martin Luther King's birthday. Now there was nothing to look forward to.

To top it off, it rained every day for two weeks. The rain was fun at first. I loved the way it sounded when it hit the windows. I liked the way it tasted on my tongue. It made the world look shiny and new.

Then everything turned to mud. Mud got into my boots. It changed my lucky red socks to brown. It splashed on my book bag. Mud even got into my hair.

"What a muddy mess! What a muddy mess! What a muddy mess!" our babysitter Mrs. Cotton kept saying. For once in my life, I agreed with Mrs. Cotton.

It was still getting dark early, too. The sun was almost gone by the time Tina and I got home from school. Every day was dull and gray. It was hard to remember how summer felt. School seemed like it would go on forever. One boring day after another.

It was Friday morning and raining again. Tomorrow would be Saturday. And it was supposed to rain then, too! It was almost time for school. Mom put out our umbrellas. Dad put out our boots and rain-coats. I wasn't looking forward to going outside.

Tina and I were eating my favorite cereal. It was the one with little round wheels that taste like honey. I usually love the way it crunches. I love how it's just a little bit sweet. But the wheels were boring today. All they did was float around in milk. Suddenly I was sick and tired of them, too.

"My life is rotten!" I said to Tina, who was reading the back of the cereal box.

"Why?" she asked, as she shoveled a spoonful of cereal into her mouth.

"There's nothing to do! Do you have any exciting ideas?"

Tina knows how to make things inter-esting, even though some of her ideas don't always work out so well. Like the time with the cookie money. I'd earned the money for the Girl Scouts of America. Then I spent it on a good cause. But Tina helped me get it back. Well, almost get it back.

And there was Tina's famous play, *The Terrific Tale of Tara, the Proud Fairy Princess*. I was the star. Well, almost the star. I had a great time, though.

"Do you have any advice?" I asked.

Tina looked at me, then put her spoon down by her plate. She took a gulp of orange juice. She swirled it around in her mouth. She threw back her head and gargled. Finally, she swallowed it.

"That is *so* gross!" I said.

Tina dug her spoon into the sugar and sprinkled it on her cereal three times.

"Sweets for the sweet!" she said. "You want advice? Here's some advice. Always add sugar. It makes everything sweet."

"But it's already sweet!" I said.

Tina's advice is never good when it comes to food. She is the only person I know who puts ketchup on tuna fish.

"So, what should I do?" I asked, crunching down on my cereal.

"About what?"

"About being sick and tired of school. Sick and tired of rain! Sick and tired of everything!"

Tina looked at me for a long time. Then she shook her head. "Well, Willie. It sounds to me like you've got a case of the middle-of-the-year blahs," she said.

"Middle-of-the-year blahs? What are those?" I asked.

"The blahs are just like they sound—
blaaaahhh! You've got to learn to look on
the bright side of things."

"Like what?"

"For one thing, it won't rain forever. The
sun will come out sooner or later. It always
does."

"What else?"

"Well, next Friday is Valentine's Day.
Valentine's Day is always fun."

I looked down at the cereal floating
around in my bowl, without saying anything.

I don't like Valentine's Day. I'm always
afraid I won't get any valentines. That is
one of my worst nightmares.

Here's how my nightmare goes: I'll be
sitting at my desk. I'll have a big smile
on my face. I'll hold out my hands, waiting

for cards. And nobody will give me a valentine. The kid next to me will get a bunch. The kid behind me will get some. But I won't get any. Not even from the teacher!

I always have a knot in my stomach

the night before Valentine's Day.

Tina looked surprised. "You're probably the only kid in the world who doesn't like Valentine's Day! Somebody always brings in those great heart-shaped candies with funny sayings. And somebody's mom bakes yummy cupcakes. Who knows, maybe this year, you might even find a secret valentine!"

"Secret valentine?"

"Stranger things have happened."

We finished our cereal and ran outside to catch our bus. I tripped and fell in the mud. As if things weren't lousy enough!

"Willie, I have some advice for you," Tina said as I wiped the mud off my raincoat. She closed her eyes and waved her hands in the air as if she were getting a psychic message. Then in a very funny voice she said: "Stay away from mud puddles, Willimena. You might fall in."

"Thanks, I'll remember that. What else?"

"Be nice to new people," she said.

"Be nice to new people? What kind of advice is that?"

"Take it or leave it," said Tina.

"I'll leave it," I said back.

But for once, my big sister was on to something.

STEP #2:
Be Nice to New People

When I got to school, I whispered good morning to the portrait of Harriet Tubman that hangs on a wall in my school. I do that every morning. But this time, Crawford Mills heard me.

"Hey, silly Willie Thomas is talking to a picture," he yelled. Wow, was that embarrassing!

The morning started out slowly. Mrs. Sweetly collected our journals. We corrected our homework. We talked about current events and read our newsmagazines.

Because it was Black History Month, Mrs. Sweetly told us that we had to do reports on our favorite black hero or heroine. We could tell her on Monday who we had chosen.

I knew who I would choose. Who else, but Harriet Tubman, my personal hero! I just hoped that nobody else would choose her too.

When it was time to go to lunch, there was a knock on the door.

"Mrs. Sweetly, could we come in for a moment?" asked Mrs. Morris, the principal. Mrs. Morris came into our class. A boy came in with her. The boy's parents were with him. The boy's dad had an arm around his shoulder. His mom had a big smile. The boy didn't.

"Mrs. Sweetly, I'd like you to meet Travis Tyler. These are his parents, Mr. and Mrs. Tyler. Travis is joining your class today," said Mrs. Morris.

Everybody stared at the new boy. He glanced around the room. He looked scared.

"I heard we were getting a new kid. That must be him," said Linda Turner, who sits next to me.

"He just moved to my block. He came

from California," said Crawford Mills.

"California! Wow, that's really far away," said Bill Taylor.

"He's really cute," said Lilac Starr. Lilac sits a couple of seats away from me. She has a loud voice.

"Class, stop whispering!" said Mrs. Sweetly. Everybody was quiet then.

I couldn't believe what the new boy was wearing. He had on a striped shirt almost like mine. We had the same brand of sneakers, too. But his had red laces. My laces are purple. We also had the same backpack. Except for his shoelaces, the new kid had good taste!

"I would like everybody to meet Travis Tyler," Mrs. Sweetly said. "He comes all the way from sunny California."

"Whoop-de-do! Sunny California!" said Crawford Mills.

"Be quiet, Crawford!" said Mrs. Sweetly in a sharp voice. She put her hands on her hips. She narrowed her eyes. Crawford looked down at his desk.

I really hoped that the new boy hadn't

heard what Crawford had said. It was bad enough to come to a new school without somebody making fun of where you came from.

"Would everybody please say hello to Travis Tyler, our new student," said Mrs. Sweetly.

"Hello, Travis Tyler," everybody said.

"I would like everyone to make a special effort today to make Travis feel welcome," Mrs. Sweetly said.

"Yes, Mrs. Sweetly," everybody said together.

"Gosh, that must really be embarrassing, a teacher forcing kids to be friendly to you," whispered Bill Taylor.

"Yeah," I said. I was starting to feel sorry for the new boy.

"He is really cute!" said Linda Turner.

I wasn't sure what "cute" meant. Sometimes I think something is cute, and nobody else does. And sometimes if I say something *isn't* cute, Tina will roll her eyes and look at me like I'm crazy.

I just hoped the new boy was friendly. "Friendly" is easy to understand. "Friendly" makes you feel good. I couldn't take another Crawford Mills in my life.

"Well, Travis, since your last name begins with a T you'll be in the T group," Mrs. Sweetly said. "You will sit between Willimena Thomas and Linda Turner."

Travis sat down between me and Linda. He looked really uncomfortable. I tried to think of something nice to say but I couldn't come up with anything. Mrs. Sweetly gave him the books that everybody else had. Then she gave him a new journal.

"What's this for?" Travis asked Bill Taylor.

"That's your journal. Everybody has one. You're supposed to write something every night," said Bill.

"Like what?" Travis asked.

"Like things that make you happy or sad. If something good happens, you can write that down. Or if somebody hurts your feelings, you can write that down, too."

"Be careful what you say, though. Mrs. Sweetly reads the journals every week," said Linda.

"It sounds like fun. I like to write!" said Travis.

"So do I!" I said.

"We have something in common," said Travis with a grin. It was the first time he had smiled. His smile made me think

Hey, that's
Harriet Tubman!

about my cousin Teddy. When Teddy grins,
everybody grins with him.

"I need two special friends to show
Travis how to get to the lunchroom, and to
show him around the school after lunch,"
Mrs. Sweetly said.

Everybody raised their hands.

Mrs. Sweetly chose me and Bill Taylor.

"Hey, that's Harriet Tubman!" Travis said when we passed by the picture of Harriet Tubman.

"The school is named for her," said Bill.

"She was really great. She was a conductor on the Underground Railroad. She never lost a passenger," said Travis.

"Harriet Tubman is my hero!" I said, then wished I hadn't said it. I hoped it didn't sound dumb.

"Really? Frederick Douglass is mine. I like reading about famous people in history," said Travis. "Do you have a favorite hero, too?" he asked Bill.

"I kind of like the Incredible Hulk," said Bill.

Although Mrs. Sweetly didn't tell us we

had to, Bill and I sat with Travis at lunch. The lunchroom can be a terrible place when you don't know anybody.

Lucky for me, my mom had packed a great lunch. It would have been awful to pull out a slimy salami or smelly egg-salad sandwich. I had peanut butter and grape jelly, orange juice, an apple, and animal crackers. Bill had bologna, grapes, chocolate cookies, and an orange. Travis had peanut butter and apple jelly, grape juice, a pear, and two granola bars.

Granola bars! One of my favorite snacks.

"Here, Willie, you want one of these? I've got two," Travis said. He must have seen my eyes light up when I saw them.

"Thanks, Travis," I said.

Travis Tyler was really a nice kid!

As we were putting our empty bags in

the trash, a familiar voice called out from across the room.

"Hey, Willie, what's going on?" she said.

"Who is that?" asked Travis.

"Tina, my big sister."

"Hey, I've got a big brother. His name is Richard. Maybe they know each other," said Travis. "Do you have any pets?"

"I've got a dog named Apple," said Bill.

"Apple!" Travis and I said at the same time. We tried not to laugh, but we couldn't help it. Bill laughed, too.

"I named him Apple because he loves to eat apples," Bill explained.

"I have a cat named Moon. Her fur is completely black. But she has one spot on her forehead shaped like a half-moon. That's why I call her Moon," said Travis.

"I have a black cat, too," I said. "He has

shiny black fur. He has a cute little nose and green eyes that glow in the dark. His name is Doofus Doolittle."

Bill and Travis laughed when I said Doofus's name, but I didn't mind. It was a funny name.

"Some people say that black cats are bad luck, but Moon is good luck," said Travis. "Is Doofus good luck, too?"

I nodded that he was. "If he were a kid, Doofus would be my best friend," I said.

"Same with Moon," said Travis.

"Well, thanks for showing me around the school," Travis said to me and Bill after we'd finished our lunch. We were heading back to Mrs. Sweetly's class.

"I'm glad you came to our school," said Bill.

"Thanks for the granola bar, and welcome to Mrs. Sweetly's class," I said, and I really meant it.

STEP #3:
WARNING: Boy + Friend = Boyfriend!

"So who was that cute boy you were sitting with in the lunchroom?" asked Tina. We were eating dinner. I had just stuffed my mouth full of macaroni and cheese. Two noodles slipped off my fork. Cheese dribbled down my chin.

"Nobody," I said.

"Don't talk with your mouth full," my mom said.

"Sorry," I said.

"He's really cute," Tina said.

Cute! There was that word again.

I filled my fork with salad and took a bite.

"What's his name?" asked Tina.

"Travis Tyler," I said.

"Willie, please don't talk with your mouth full," my mom said again.

I chewed my food and swallowed it. "Mrs. Sweetly asked me and Bill to show him around."

"Travis Tyler? Does he live around here?" my dad asked.

"How do I know!" I said. It sounded fresh, but it was too late to change it. I didn't like where this conversation was going. I didn't want to talk about the new boy. Especially not to my parents and my nosy sister.

"Willie, don't be fresh," my mom said.

I took a gulp of juice.

"Does he sit next to you in Mrs. Sweetly's class?" asked Tina.

"None of your beeswax!" I said.

"Willie has a boyfriend! Willie has a boyfriend! Willie has a boyfriend!" Tina said in a singsong voice.

"No, I don't."

"Yes, you do!"

"Shut up, Tina!" I said.

"Mom, Willie told me to shut up!" Tina said.

"No fighting at the table," my dad said.

"I'm not fighting, I just want Tina to leave me alone," I said.

"Well, does he?" Tina asked again.

"Does he what?"

"Sit next to you?"

"His name starts with T like mine," I said.

"Something in common!" Tina said.

"May I be excused?" I left the table as fast as I could. I didn't feel like hearing anything else Tina had to say.

Even though it was Friday night, I decided to do my homework early. There's a first for everything. The truth was, I didn't want Tina to tease me anymore. I also wanted to read about Harriet Tubman for my report.

When I sat down on my bed, Doofus Doolittle jumped up on me. He licked my face. I think he smelled the cheese. That made me laugh.

"You are my good-luck charm, Doofus!" I said, and gave him a hug. Then, I remembered that that was what Travis had said about Moon, his black cat. I sure didn't want Tina to know that Travis had a black cat, too. She would never stop teasing me.

I looked up Harriet Tubman in my book on African American heroes. I never got tired of reading about her and what she had done. I thought about what Travis had said about Frederick Douglass. I looked up his name, too. Frederick Douglass was born at almost the same time as Harriet Tubman. And he fought against slavery, too.

Tina came into our room and bounced on my bed. "What are you doing?" she asked.

"Studying." I was still mad at her for teasing me about Travis.

"It's Friday, don't study now!"

"I want to," I said.

"I'm sorry I said that about you and Travis," she said, settling down next to me.

She picked Doofus Doolittle up and kissed his nose.

"That's okay," I said.

"But Travis is a boy, right? He is a friend, right?"

I thought for a minute. "I don't know yet. He's really nice. Maybe we will be friends."

"Well, doesn't that make him your boyfriend?" Tina asked. She had a smile on her face. She was still trying to tease me! "Well, doesn't it?"

"No," I said. "And I don't want to talk about this anymore." Tina knew I meant it this time.

"Dad made some popcorn. If you come downstairs, I'll give you more than half," she said.

That was a big deal coming from Tina.

Then she added, "Anyway, it's more important that Travis is a friend than a boy.
Maybe Travis is a *friendboy*."

That sounded good. "Okay, I'll be down
in a minute," I said.

Before I went downstairs, I wrote in my
journal.

A new boy came into my class. Everyone
thinks he is cute, but I think he is really
friendly. That's more important. His name is
Travis Tyler. I hope we can be friends.

Then I wrote,

BUT HE IS NOT MY BOYFRIEND!

I wrote that in big letters and drew a
line under *not*. Just in case Tina read it.

STEP #4:
Tighten the Knot in Your Stomach

"We have two important things to talk about today," Mrs. Sweetly said on Monday morning.

I knew what one thing was, and I was ready for that. I knew exactly who I was going to write my Black History report on.

"Does everyone know what day Friday is?" Mrs. Sweetly asked.

"Valentine's Day!" shouted Lilac Starr. "My favorite holiday!"

"Yes, Lilac, you're right. Friday is Valentine's Day."

"My mother is making chocolate cupcakes for the whole class!" said Lilac.

"My mom said she'd bring in candy," said Bill Taylor.

"My mom's not doing nothing," said Crawford Mills. Everybody laughed when he said that. Except Mrs. Sweetly.

"Since your mom's not doing *anything*, Crawford, you can volunteer to work on the valentine box," she said.

"Aaauugh!" Crawford groaned. He sunk down into his seat.

"I will need three more volunteers," Mrs. Sweetly said. "The people who volunteer will have to be creative. They have to love art. They should like to draw, because they will have to come up with a design."

"But I hate art!" said Crawford. Mrs. Sweetly ignored him.

Lilac raised her hand. Then Travis raised his hand. He said he would like to help, too.

"Hey, don't do that. Art is girl stuff!" Bill whispered to Travis.

"That's not true. My dad is an artist. And I love to draw," Travis said.

He was right about that. Travis had decorated the cover of his journal with beautiful designs. He had drawn them with red, blue, and yellow pencils.

"Did you draw that?" I asked when I saw it.

Travis nodded that he did. He looked very proud.

Mrs. Sweetly looked in my direction. "Would you like to volunteer, Willie?" she asked.

I scrunched down in my seat and shook my head.

"Then I need somebody else!" said Mrs. Sweetly.

"I'd like to help," said Linda Turner. She smiled at Travis. "I love to draw, too," she said. That wasn't true! Linda hated art almost as much as Crawford did.

"The children who are going to design the box can start this afternoon. We can start bringing in our valentines tomorrow morning."

Everybody started to cheer. Except me. That old worry knot was back.

"And now I'd like everybody to tell me who you will be writing your Black History report on," Mrs. Sweetly said. "We will start with the A group. Janet Anderson?" she said, taking out a notebook and nodding in Janet's direction.

"Harriet Tubman."

"Patricia Andrews?"

"Harriet Tubman."

"John Allen?"

"Harriet Tubman."

Three kids were doing my personal hero, and we hadn't even gotten to the B group!

By the time Mrs. Sweetly got to S, so many kids had picked Harriet Tubman that she said nobody else could choose her. I was out of luck! I couldn't think of anybody else except Frederick Douglass, Travis's hero. But almost as many kids had chosen Frederick Douglass as had picked Harriet Tubman.

Finally, Mrs. Sweetly got to me.

"Whom do you choose, Willie? Whom are you going to write about?" she asked.

"I don't know," I said. All the heroes that I knew had been picked by other kids.

Mrs. Sweetly sighed. "Children who do not have a hero will have to go to the library and find a new one," she said. "There are always new heroes to discover."

I'd really been looking forward to writing about Harriet Tubman, even though I already knew a lot about her. But maybe it wouldn't be so bad to find somebody new. Besides, I loved to go to the library. Mrs. Knapp, our librarian, was one of the nicest grown-ups in the school. She was happy to see me whenever I went to the library. I was always happy to see her, too.

"Who in the class needs a new hero to write about?" Mrs. Sweetly asked. Travis and I were the only kids in the T group to raise our hands. Mrs. Sweetly said that we could be library partners. I was glad Tina wasn't around to hear that. She would have teased me forever. After we finished lunch, Mrs. Sweetly sent us to the library to find new heroes.

When we got to the library, Mrs. Knapp

gave me and Travis reference books about black history. I sat on a yellow cushion and slowly looked through my book. Finally, I found someone. Her name was Zora Neale Hurston. I liked her because she had a name that was different. You don't meet a lot of people named Zora, just like you don't meet a lot of people named Willimena. When Zora was a kid, she liked to tell stories, just like me. Sometimes she got into trouble, too. I was glad to read that.

I went to the front of the room where Mrs. Knapp kept the books about famous Americans. Just my luck. Somebody had gotten there first.

"That young man over there has all the books," said Mrs. Knapp. She pointed to Travis. He was sitting at one of the tables, surrounded by a pile of books.

"Why don't you ask him if he will share?" said Mrs. Knapp.

"Do you have a hero yet?" he asked when I sat down.

"Zora Neale Hurston," I said. "Do you have one?"

"Langston Hughes. Both their last names start with H. They're on the same page." He pointed to a picture of Zora Neale Hurston.

Suddenly I remembered something important. "I know who Langston Hughes is," I said. "My dad has a book of poems that he wrote."

"That's great!" said Travis. "Do you think he'll let me borrow it? Maybe I can copy down one for my report."

"I'm sure he will," I said.

Travis was really nice about sharing.

He gave me half of the reference books. I was glad that I had to share with him instead of Crawford Mills.

After we were finished, Mrs. Knapp signed our library passes so that we could go back to Mrs. Sweetly's class. I stopped in the girls' room on the way back.

As I was washing my hands, Lilac Starr and Linda Turner came in. They were so busy talking about Valentine's Day they didn't notice I was there.

"Don't you just love Valentine's Day!" said Lilac. "I always get so many valentines. I always get more than I send. Valentine's Day is the best thing that happens to me all year!"

"I think I'm going to get a special card from somebody this year," said Linda.

"I think I will too," said Lilac. "Aren't

you happy we're working on the valentine box with Travis Tyler? He is *so* cute."

"He was really nice to me when we started working together," said Linda. "I hope I will be his special valentine."

"Well, I hate to say this, but I am going to be his special valentine. He gave me his cupcake today at lunch," said Lilac. I could tell by her voice that she didn't really hate to say it.

"But he shared his colored pencils with me. He told me a secret. He said he wants to be an artist some day," said Linda.

"You must be wrong. Travis told me he wanted to be a historian when he grows up," said Lilac.

Finally they saw me.

"Hi, Willie," they both said together.

Then they forgot I was there.

"Don't worry. You always get the most cards in the whole class," said Linda.

"I know," said Lilac.

"Don't you feel sorry for people who don't get any valentines?" asked Linda. "There's always somebody in the class who only gets one or two."

The knot in my stomach returned.

"That must be so-o-o embarrassing," said Lilac.

They both started to laugh.

"I wonder who will be embarrassed this year?" said Linda.

I quickly left the girls' room without saying anything. I just hoped it wouldn't be me! But the knot in my stomach was getting tighter by the minute.

STEP #5:
Take Bad Advice from Your Dumb Sister

Valentine's Day was coming fast. There was nothing I could do to stop it. The valentine box was covered with bright red paper. Long white streamers ran down its sides. Travis drew fancy designs on the front. Lilac and Linda cut hearts out of lacy paper and hung them on the back. Crawford wrote "Happy Valentine's Day" on the top. He misspelled "Happy" and "Valentine's." It said: "hapy valentine's day." But nobody seemed to care.

On Tuesday morning, kids started bringing in their valentines. The box was in the back of the room. It was in the same place where Lester's cage used to be. Lester was our class guinea pig. He escaped from his cage and disappeared when I took him home one weekend. It was one of the worst days of my life.

I was probably the only kid in the whole class who remembered Lester. Nobody talked about him anymore. These days, everybody was busy talking about Travis Tyler. In less than a week, Travis had become the Romeo of Mrs. Sweetly's class.

All the girls liked Travis. Everybody wanted a special valentine from him. Everybody thought she was going to be the only girl to get one. In the girls' room, Valentine's Day and Travis Tyler were the only things anyone talked about.

"I know Travis Tyler is going to give me the biggest valentine," I heard Jane say to Dana.

"Travis Tyler shared his cupcake with me, and he gave me the biggest piece. I know I'm going to be his special valentine," Sally said to Joyce.

"Travis let me get in front of him when we were in line for the water fountain," said Anne to Louisa.

"I'm saving my prettiest valentine for Travis Tyler," said Lilac. "I know he's saving one for me!"

"Don't be so sure about that!" said Linda.

But Travis was nice to everybody. He always let kids get in front of him in line. He always shared his cookies and cupcakes. After I loaned him my dad's book on Langston Hughes, he brought me a granola bar. But I didn't think that made me his special valentine. I just thought he was a nice kid who wanted to be everybody's friend.

By Thursday morning, the valentine box was filled to the top. Soon there would be no more room. I hadn't brought my cards to school yet. I hadn't written any. I was waiting until the last minute. Thursday night was the last minute.

That night, I pulled out the three boxes of valentines my mom had bought. There were enough cards for everybody in my class and lots of extras in case I made mistakes. Just as I picked up my pencil to write, a bunch of what-ifs popped into my head.

What if nobody sent me any cards?

What if I was the only kid in the room not to get any?

What if everybody made fun of me?

I felt the old night-before-Valentine's Day knot forming in my stomach.

"What's wrong, Willie? You look worried,"

Tina said when she came into our room. Then she saw what I was doing. "You haven't finished writing your cards! That's terrible, Willie. Tomorrow is Valentine's Day!"

"But I told you how I feel about Valentine's Day," I said.

What's wrong, Willie?

"Tell me again."

"I hate it. I'm scared I won't get any cards."

"But you always get cards!"

"What if this year is different?"

"Well, if you're really that scared, why don't you just send a valentine to yourself?" Tina suggested.

"Is that fair?" Somehow that didn't seem right.

"At least you know you'll get one," Tina said.

Maybe Tina was right, I thought. Who said I couldn't send a valentine to myself? I could say it was to somebody very special. And I was very special. My mom always said that.

So I wrote: *To Willie Thomas, A Very Special Person!* on an envelope. I picked out a fancy valentine. I signed it: *A Secret Admirer.*

Well, I did admire me sometimes. And I didn't tell anyone!

Then I wrote valentines out for the kids in my class. I picked out really pretty ones for Travis, Bill, Linda, and my other friends. I even picked out a nice one for Crawford Mills.

But when I signed the last card, I had a terrible thought.

What if the card I sent myself was the only one I got?

Silly Willie Thomas only got one card! Ha! Ha! Ha! I could almost hear Crawford Mills teasing me.

Maybe I should write another one just in case, I thought. At least, I'd get two.

But what if I only got two?

If I could send two cards, why not four?

Why not six? Why not ten?

So I wrote all the cards that were left to myself. I used different colored pencils so nobody would know it was from the same person.

When I was finished, I counted them. There were cards for all the kids in my class—plus a lot of extra ones that said *To Willie Thomas, A Very Special Person*, just in case. I grinned as I sealed them up. I didn't have to worry now. I'd get plenty of cards. The old worry knot was gone.

"Thanks, Tina," I said as I stuffed them into my backpack.

"You can always count on me to come up with a good idea," Tina said.

Another great idea from my dear big sister.

Now, that should have been a warning!

STEP #6:
Stuff the Valentine Box

When I got to school the next day, everybody was excited. We had a substitute teacher.

"Good morning, children. I'm Miss Lacey," the new teacher said. She looked very young, almost like a teenager. She also looked scared. Everybody started talking at once.

"Quiet down, children. I expect you to behave," she said. A couple of kids giggled. Miss Lacey looked surprised, but she kept smiling.

It was starting off to be a great day. It's always fun to have a substitute teacher. There was also going to be a party, so we would have double fun! This was going to be my best Valentine's Day ever. I was sure of that.

But a scary thing happened on the way to the valentine box. I dropped some cards on the floor. Two were written in red pencil. The others were written in blue. They all said: *To Willie Thomas, A Very Special Person*.

Just my luck, Crawford Mills picked them up. He looked at them. He looked at me. Then he dropped them in the box.

"Thanks, Crawford," I said, feeling a little nervous.

"No problem, Willie," he said, but he looked puzzled.

Miss Lacey said we would have the Valentine's Day party at the end of the day. Everybody began to cheer. It was going to be hard to wait.

After lunch, our class went to see a play given by the fifth graders. When we were getting into line, Dana and Jeanne started to argue. They were fighting about who was going to stand next to Travis.

"I was here first," said Dana.

"No, I was," said Jeanne.

Miss Lacey told them to stop.

"You can't tell me what to do, you're not my teacher," Jeanne said.

Miss Lacey looked puzzled. She didn't know what to say. Everybody started to giggle. But, finally, the fighting stopped.

I could tell Travis was really embarrassed. I was sure he hated being the center of attention. It wasn't his fault that all the girls liked him.

The play wasn't very good. None of the fifth graders remembered their lines. They kept glancing at the cue cards they all had in their pockets. Our class acted up. Kids clapped when they weren't supposed to. A couple of boys laughed when the actors said sad things. Maybe everybody was too excited about Valentine's Day to sit still and behave.

I felt sorry for Miss Lacey. I could tell she felt bad. When she told everybody to be quiet, nobody listened. We all ran down the hall back to our classroom. Miss Lacey ran behind us trying to keep up.

Finally, we were back in our room. Lilac's and Bill's mothers had placed red napkins on everyone's desks. There were big chocolate cupcakes on each napkin. Paper cups of apple juice were next to the cupcakes. Candy hearts were next to the juice. It was time for the party!

"Can we have more cupcakes when we're finished?" asked Crawford Mills.

Miss Lacey looked a little nervous. "I guess it's okay," she said. Everybody began to cheer. We all ate our cupcakes quickly so we could get seconds.

I was having a great time. Everybody was laughing. Everybody was talking at once. Everybody was being nice to everybody else.

"I'm so happy that you're my friend," Linda said to me. "I hope you like the valentine I sent you."

"Thank you!" I said. "I hope you like my card, too." I tried to remember the card I'd

sent Linda. I hoped it was one of the pretty ones. I hoped I hadn't sent them all to myself.

"I sent you a really nice valentine, too," said Bill. "You're one of the nicest kids in the whole class."

"Wow, thanks, Bill," I said. That was one of the kindest things anyone had ever said to me. I hoped I'd given Bill a nice card, too. Trouble was, I couldn't remember!

"Yeah, Willie, you really are a good kid," said Travis.

I nodded. I had more friends than I thought. Maybe I didn't need to send all those cards to myself, after all.

"I sent all the girls my prettiest cards, except one," said Dana. "I sent that to a special boy in the class."

"Me, too," said Jeanne.

I glanced at Travis. I wondered if he knew that a lot of girls had sent him special valentines.

I wondered if I remembered to send him one. I hoped that I had. Then I had a terrible thought. What if I'd forgotten to send cards to everybody? I got a queasy feeling in my stomach. And it wasn't from the cupcakes.

Finally, it was the moment everyone had been waiting for. Since Miss Lacey didn't know our names, she asked Lilac if she would help pass out the valentines.

Lilac opened the box and got out the valentines.

"I want everybody in the whole class to be my valentine," said Charley, who sits in Crawford's group. "I hope everybody likes the cards I gave them."

Soon everybody's desk was piling up with cards. Everyone was thanking everybody else.

After a while, it seemed like every card Lilac passed out was to me. For every card she gave somebody else, I got two. My pile of cards got bigger and bigger. They all said the same thing: *To Willie Thomas, A Very Special Person.*

Soon, the only cards being passed out were my cards to myself. They were the only ones left. Lilac's frown grew bigger and bigger. My neck felt hot. I wished the cards would stop coming.

Finally, Lilac had passed out all the cards. I breathed a sigh of relief. When she sat down to open her cards, she glanced at my desk. Her frown turned to a scowl.

"Thank you, Travis!" said Linda. She held up the card Travis had given her. It was a picture of a cute little frog. The frog had on a black top hat. He was holding a big red valentine.

Would You Be My Valentine? it said in silver letters.

"Hey, wait a minute, that's the same card Travis gave me!" said Lilac.

"Me, too!" said Dana, holding up her card. "Who wants a yucky frog holding a valentine?"

"Travis gave me the same disgusting card!" said Jeanne.

Everyone started opening their cards from Travis.

They were all frogs in top hats holding valentines.

They all said *Would You Be My Valentine?* in silver letters.

They were all signed, *From your friend, Travis Tyler*.

"I thought I was your special valentine," said Linda.

"I thought *I* was your special valentine!" yelled Lilac.

"Traitor!" said Dawn.

"Cheater!" said Jeanne.

"I'm not going to be your friend anymore," said Lilac. She stood up. She took the card Travis had given her. She threw it into the trash. Then she stomped back to her seat.

"Hey, don't do that," said Miss Lacey. But it was too late. Janis was already doing the same thing. So were Dana, Jeanne, and Linda.

"Sit down, everybody!" said Miss Lacey.

But nobody listened. All the girls were talking. Everybody was running to the trash can. When it was time for us to throw away our napkins and paper cups, the trash was overflowing with Travis's cards.

Travis looked like he was going to cry. Everybody was mad at him, except me.

I had troubles of my own.

STEP #7:
Do the Math

"Hey, look at all the valentines Willie got! She got more cards than anybody else." yelled Linda. I glanced at my desk. I had two huge piles of valentines. I had so many cards, some had fallen on the floor. I started to count them. There were 48. I quickly did the math. I counted 25 cards from the kids in my class. Could it be that I had sent myself 23 valentines? I counted again. I was right. There were 23 cards from "A Secret Admirer." And there were 25 cards from everyone else.

"Congratulations, Willie!" said Jane. "You're the most popular kid in the room."

"Maybe in the whole school!" said Chris.

Everybody had forgotten about Travis Tyler. I was suddenly the center of attention. Everyone gathered around my desk.

"You're really lucky, Willie. Everybody must have sent you two cards. I wish somebody had sent me two cards," Bill said sadly. I looked at the pile of cards on his desk. There weren't that many there. I had twice as many as he did.

"Did you get cards from kids in other classes?" asked Dana. She looked suspicious.

I didn't want to tell a lie, so I shrugged my shoulders. Shrugging my shoulders could mean maybe I did. It could mean maybe I didn't. It could also mean I didn't know. I hadn't lied, but I felt like I had. Suddenly, I didn't feel so good.

Lilac Starr came over to my desk. She stared at the pile of cards on my desk. She had a sad look on her face. I could tell she was disappointed because I'd gotten more cards than she did.

I remembered what Lilac had said about Valentine's Day in the girls' room. It was her favorite holiday. It was the best thing that happened to her all year. It wasn't really important to me, not like it was to Lilac.

But sometimes Lilac made me mad. She could be mean to other people. I didn't like the way she always had to be the first person in line. And I didn't like the way she threw Travis's card in the trash. But I knew how it felt to be sad. I didn't want anyone to feel that way, not even Lilac Starr.

I wished I hadn't taken Tina's advice. I wished I hadn't been so worried.

But it was too late for wishes. Crawford Mills was heading in my direction.

He came over to my desk and picked up one of my cards. He looked at it carefully. Then he picked up another card. Then Crawford looked at me with a scowl on his face.

"That's not fair, Willie," he said in a quiet voice.

"What's not fair?" asked Bill and Linda together.

"Ask Willie," said Crawford. "I don't like people to snitch on me, so I don't snitch on anybody else."

"What does he mean?" asked Lilac.

I took a deep breath. I tried hard to shrug my shoulders. But they were frozen stiff.

Then Lilac stepped forward. She picked up two of my cards and read them. They were both from "A Secret Admirer."

"What does 'secret admirer' mean?" she asked.

"Somebody who secretly admires you," said Bill.

Lilac handed Linda the cards without saying anything.

"You sure do have a bunch of secret admirers, Willie," Linda said after she'd read them.

The moment of truth was here.

"No," I said in a quiet voice. "I only have one."

"What do you mean one?" everybody asked at once.

"My 'secret admirer' is me," I said in a small voice.

"Do you mean you sent all these cards to yourself?" asked Bill. His eyes were big, as if he couldn't believe I'd done it.

"But why?" asked Linda.

"Because I didn't think I'd get any valentines," I said.

"Then you really didn't get all those cards?" asked Lilac. "That's cheating! You were trying to fool everybody in the class."

"No, I wasn't!" I said.

"That means I got more cards than you, after all," Lilac said.

It would have been better if everybody had just laughed. Or yelled at me. Or called me names. But nobody did. Everyone just stared at me without saying anything.

Then Bill spoke. "Willie, you're in our class. Everybody likes you. Look at all of the cards you got from us."

I nodded and looked at the pile of cards from the class. Bill was right.

Of course, Crawford Mills had to have the last word.

"That was a dumb thing to do, Willie Thomas," he said.

What could I say? He was right!

I had managed to do a dumb thing twenty-three times.

Finally, the party was over and it was time to go home. Miss Lacey passed out our journals. I knew what I was going to write in mine. Kids started packing up their books and notebooks. Everybody was still in a good mood. Except me.

I shoved all my cards into my backpack without looking at them. When I got home, I'd throw away all the ones I'd written to myself. Then read the real ones from the kids at school.

I waited for a long time to get my coat and boots. I was too embarrassed to get in line with everybody else. I wanted to be the last person to leave. So I sat at my desk and wrote in my journal:

Another lousy Valentine's Day. And it's my own fault!
I found 23 ways to mess it up.

Then I added,

I really missed Mrs. Sweetly today. We really, really needed her. I hope she will come back to school on Monday.

There were only two other people left in

the room when I finished writing in my journal. One was Miss Lacey, the substitute teacher. The other person was Travis Tyler. I'd been so worried about myself, I'd forgotten all about him. He had his head on his desk. I wondered if he had been crying.

STEP #8:
Get Ready to Be
SURPRISED!

"Travis, are you okay?" I asked him.

"I wasn't crying," he said. "I just wanted to put my head on my desk."

"If you were crying it would be okay. Everybody cries when they feel bad," I said.

"But I wasn't crying!" he said. "I sure hope nobody thought I was crying!" I knew he had seen everybody throw his valentines in the trash. That would be enough to make anybody cry.

"I don't think anybody noticed that you had your head on your desk," I said. "Everybody was paying too much attention to me."

Travis started to gather up his books and pile them into his backpack. As we passed Mrs. Sweetly's desk, Miss Lacey glanced up.

"Good night, children," she said.

"Good night, Miss Lacey," Travis and I said together.

"Wanna walk to the bus together?" Travis asked in the hallway.

"Okay," I said.

I glanced at Harriet Tubman's picture as we walked past. It always made me feel stronger when I remembered all the things that had happened to her. When I thought about what she'd gone through,

Valentine's Day didn't seem very important.

"I didn't mean to hurt everybody's feelings," Travis said after a minute. "I just
wanted to be friendly."

"But how come you gave everybody the
same valentine?" I asked.

"Those were the only cards I had," he
said. "I didn't know everybody would be
mad because they were the same." He gave
a long, sad sigh. "I love frogs. I don't think
they're yucky. I thought everybody else
would like them too. Don't you like frogs?"

"Not particularly," I said. "But the top
hats were cute."

"Can I ask you something, Willie?"

"Sure."

"How come you sent yourself all those
cards?"

"I wanted to make sure I got some valentines. I guess I just got carried away," I said.

"Yeah, I'd say," Travis said, smiling. It was the first time he had smiled since the party. It was the first time I had smiled, too.

We walked a little farther, not talking much. But it was nice walking with someone to the bus.

"I really hope nobody thought I was crying," Travis said again. "I don't want people to think I'm a crybaby."

"Well, even if they did, everybody will have forgotten it by Monday, anyway," I said. I thought about Lester, the class guinea pig, and how quickly everyone forgot him.

"I hope so," Travis said.

For WILLIMENA

Thank you for being my new friend.

Happy Valentine's Day

from Travis E. Tyler

Just as Travis was about to get on his bus, he stopped.

"Oh yeah, Willie. I forgot to give one person a valentine." He handed me a big white envelope addressed to Willie Thomas. "This is for you," he said. Then he ran onto the bus without looking back.

I opened Travis's valentine when I got home.

He had made it himself. It was a drawing of a black cat with a white patch on her face shaped like a half-moon. She looked the way I thought Moon, Travis's cat, must look. She was holding a big red valentine.

Thank you for being my new friend.
Happy Valentine's Day
from Travis E. Tyler

was printed in white and green letters.

"Thanks, Travis," I said, even though I knew he couldn't hear me.

Just then, Tina came into our room and bounced down on my bed. "So, how did it go today?" she asked.

"Not great," I said.

"Didn't you get any valentines?" She looked worried.

"I got enough," I said. I didn't feel like sharing all the terrible details yet.

"So my idea worked!"

"More or less," I said.

"So tell me the truth, do you have a secret valentine?" I could tell Tina really wanted to know.

But I just smiled. As far as my nosy big sister was concerned, my secret valentine was going to stay a secret.

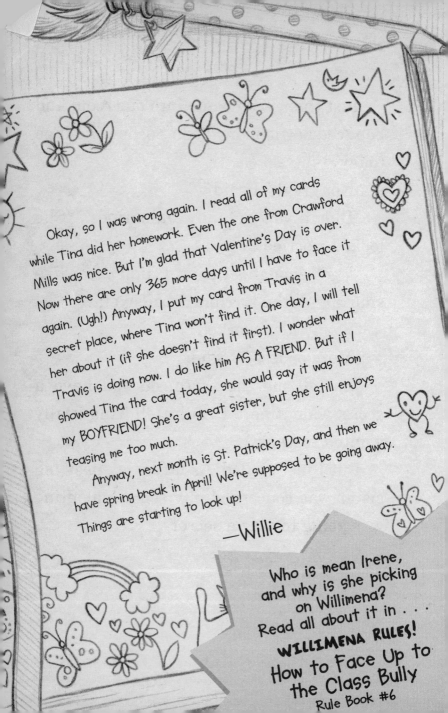

Okay, so I was wrong again. I read all of my cards while Tina did her homework. Even the one from Crawford Mills was nice. But I'm glad that Valentine's Day is over. Now there are only 365 more days until I have to face it again. (Ugh!) Anyway, I put my card from Travis in a secret place, where Tina won't find it. One day, I will tell her about it (if she doesn't find it first). I wonder what Travis is doing now. I do like him AS A FRIEND. But if I showed Tina the card today, she would say it was from my BOYFRIEND! She's a great sister, but she still enjoys teasing me too much.

Anyway, next month is St. Patrick's Day, and then we have spring break in April! We're supposed to be going away. Things are starting to look up!

—Willie

Who is mean Irene, and why is she picking on Willimena? Read all about it in . . .

WILLIMENA RULES!
How to Face Up to the Class Bully
Rule Book #6